WONDRY FINDS A HOME

THE ADVENTURES OF WONDRY DRAGON

JOAN MARIE VERBA

FTL PUBLICATIONS
MINNEAPOLIS, MINNESOTA

Copyright © 2016 by Joan Marie Verba

FTL Publications
P O Box 22693
Minneapolis, MN 55422
www.ftlpublications.com
mail@ftlpublications.com

Cover and interior dragon artwork by Jacob Richards
Cover and interior artwork copyright © 2016 by FTL Publications

Printed in the United States of America

ISBN 978-1-936881-44-4

All rights reserved.

This is a work of fiction. The names, characters, and places are products of the author's imagination. Any resemblance to actual persons, living or dead, is entirely coincidental.

Chapter 1

Rhea Monroe looked out the window as her mother parked the car at the animal shelter. After Rhea got out, her mother touched her arm.

"Remember, your father is allergic, so no dogs, cats, or birds."

Rhea sighed. "I know, Mom."

"And if we don't find another animal, we have to go home without, understand?"

Rhea nodded. "I know, Mom."

Mom smiled. "Okay, let's go in."

Rhea rushed in, without waiting for her mother to catch up. Right away, she heard barking, mewing, and cawing sounds.

A woman in a red shirt and blue jeans walked up and leaned down. "You must be Rhea."

She smiled. "Yes."

The woman straightened up. "And you must be Ms. Monroe."

Rhea turned to see her mother behind her.

Her mother held out a hand to the woman. "Heather," she said.

"Ingrid," said the woman, and they shook hands. "Now, let's see, you said no dogs or cats or birds over the phone . . . ."

"What else do you have?" Mom asked.

Ingrid led the way past cages where dogs and cats watched them curiously. "We have some rabbits, hamsters, and even a chinchilla." She took them to the back where they saw smaller cages.

Mom shook her head. "Rhea's Dad is allergic to those, too. Do you have any animals without fur or feathers?"

Before Ingrid could answer, they heard another sound.

"Trrryl, trrryl, trrryl."

Rhea put her head up. "What's that?"

"That's our dragon," Ingrid said.

Rhea's mother frowned. "Dragon? I thought dragons only lived in woods and fields, away from people."

Ingrid led them to a cage near the back door. "Well, we don't see them often. Usually the dragon mothers come from wherever the dragons live and lay their eggs in a field. Farmers look after the young dragons until they get older, grow wings, and fly back to wherever dragon land is."

"How long before that happens?" Mom asked.

"About ten to fifteen years," Ingrid said.

"Rhea would be just about starting college," Mom said.

Rhea stood in front of the cage. The dragon stood about as tall as she was with its head up and all four paws on the ground. The legs were short and stubby. The body was long and thick and was covered with golden-brown scales. There was a ridge going down its back from its head to the end of its tail. It stomped its feet and stretched its neck. Rhea put her hand to the cage so the dragon would sniff it.

"It seems excited," Mom said.

"It's a 'she,'" Ingrid answered.

"Trrryl, trrryl, trrryl," the dragon said.

"She sounds like a bird," Rhea said.

"Don't dragons roar?" Mom asked.

"The grownup ones do," Ingrid said, "and sometimes the younger ones will, if they think something's going to hurt them."

Rhea turned to Ingrid. "Does she have a name?"

Ingrid shook her head. "The farmer who brought her in never named her. He just kept her around because dragons eat mice and voles and other pests that destroy the crops. But the farmer retired and sold his land to a house builder. He didn't need her anymore."

"Does she start fires?" Mom said.

"No, they don't breathe fire until they grow up and have wings."

"What do they eat?" Mom asked. "Besides mice, that is."

"Oh, dragons will eat almost everything. They're tough inside and out. They'll eat dirt and rocks. It's good for their digestion. They'll eat bones—like the soup bones you get from the supermarket."

"Do they eat cookies?" Rhea had stuck her hand inside the cage. The dragon smelled it.

Ingrid laughed. "Yes, they'll eat anything, but they don't like cookies and cakes as much as humans do. They love flowers, though. It's like candy to them."

"Do they eat roses?" Mom asked.

Ingrid nodded. "Thorns and all. As I said, they're tough inside. They don't get sick, either."

Mom watched as the dragon pushed against Rhea's hand with its nose. "Do they bite?"

"Not unless it's something they want to eat. They're kind to people who are nice to them."

"Do they puddle on the carpet?" Mom asked.

"No, dragons keep their nests clean, and their home is their nest. They like to go in the bushes. And if they need to go, they'll pound on the door until you let them out."

"We have bushes, Mom," Rhea said.

"Their droppings make good fertilizer," Ingrid said.

Mom bent down to inspect the dragon's feet. "Is she going to claw the furniture?"

"The claws retract when she walks, though you might hear a little click on the floor. They come out only when the dragon wants to grab something to eat. She sharpens them on rocks, not wood or fabric."

Mom turned to Rhea. "What do you think of the dragon?"

"I like her, Mom. I think she likes me."

Mom straightened up and faced Ingrid. "Okay, we'll take her."

Ingrid opened the cage. The dragon hurried out. Rhea hugged the dragon's neck. The dragon trilled happily.

Holding one of the dragon's back ridges, Ingrid led them all to her office, where she filled out a form on the computer. "What do want to name her?" she asked Rhea.

"Wondry, because she's wonderful."

Ingrid printed the form. Mom paid the fee and signed the papers. Ingrid used a machine that sort of looked like a stapler to stamp a tag. She put the tag on a collar and put the collar around

Wondry's neck. Then she took what appeared to be a small gun and pulled back a scale behind one of Wondry's shoulders. She pushed the gun against Wondry's skin and squeezed the trigger. It made a noise like a cap gun, but Wondry did not seem to mind at all.

"Microchip in case you ever lose her," Ingrid said.

The next step was getting Wondry in the car. Rhea thought that might be difficult, but when they opened the back door, Wondry climbed right in. Rhea got into her booster seat and put on the seat belt. Wondry flopped onto the seat next to Rhea and put her head in Rhea's lap for the drive home.

Chapter 2

Mom drove the car right into the garage and closed the garage door so Wondry would not run out. Rhea's father opened the door from the garage to the house and stepped out. "What did you get?"

Rhea unbuckled her seat belt and opened the door. Wondry charged out.

Her father leaned back. "Okay. That's either the strangest alligator I ever saw or something else."

"It's a dragon, Dad," Rhea said.

"A dragon?" Dad said as Wondry ambled up to him and sniffed his hand.

"Yes, her name is Wondry," Rhea said.

Dad knelt in front of Wondry and rubbed her long neck. "Well, you're a good girl, aren't you?"

"Trrryl, trrryl, trrryl," Wondry replied.

Dad stood and took a step back. "That's a strange noise for a dragon to make."

"That's how she talks, Dad," Rhea said.

"Let's get her inside," Mom said.

They all stood in the dining area, next to the kitchen. Mom put her purse on the closet shelf and turned. "All right. We can make a place for Wondry in a corner, under the window. Rhea, you promised you would take care of whatever pet we got. We can use the old blankets from the upstairs closet."

Rhea walked up the stairs and opened the linen closet. Wondry followed and watched as Rhea grabbed a stack of old blankets. They went back downstairs. Rhea put the blankets in a corner. Wondry started using her feet and claws to push them around.

"Now you need to get a water bowl for Wondry," Mom said.

"There's a clean plastic bucket in the basement," Dad said. "You can fill it with the laundry tub faucet."

Rhea found the bucket downstairs and filled it with water. It was too heavy to carry, so she poured out about half and hauled it up the stairs. She put it next to where Wondry kept pushing the blankets around. Right away, Wondry put her head in the bucket and drank noisily, splashing water all over the floor.

Mom sighed. "You'll have to get some old towels, too, and wipe up the water. Leave the towels under the bucket. It seems Wondry is a messy drinker."

Dad, who had sat in a chair watching, stood and took the bucket. "I'll fill this up again while you get the towels."

Rhea came back with the towels and wiped up the floor as Wondry drank all the water that Dad had brought. He picked up the bucket again. "You're a thirsty girl."

After four buckets, Wondry finally stopped drinking. She pushed the blankets around again as Rhea wiped up the remaining water from the floor. Then Rhea layered several towels on the floor and put the bucket in the middle of the top layer.

Wondry finished making her nest with the blankets and settled on them, curling around so her head and tail nearly met.

"Well, that's a start," Mom said.

Rhea went upstairs to her bedroom to get a book. This time, Wondry did not follow her. When she came back down, Rhea sat in the circle Wondry had made with her body and leaned against Wondry's side. Wondry was nice and warm. She started reading the book out loud to Wondry and not long after, Wondry fell asleep.

Wondry was still asleep when they sat down to supper. When chickens had been on sale at the store, they had bought a bunch and put them in the freezer. While Dad cut up and fried one of the chickens, Mom heated another chicken in the microwave. Mom had Rhea get an old chipped serving plate from the cupboard. They put the microwaved chicken on it and set it next to Wondry. "We'll also put our chicken bones there for Wondry to eat when we're finished," Mom said.

Rhea sat down to eat. She heard a loud crunching noise. Looking down, she saw Wondry biting off pieces of chicken and munching them, bones and all. When she and her parents had finished eating, Rhea scraped the bones from their plates onto the platter. Wondry ate those, too, grabbing them with her toes and putting them in her mouth. The toes bent and unbent almost like fingers.

As Rhea put the plates and silverware in the dishwasher, Dad said, "We need to take Wondry outside and see if she needs to go."

When they had cleaned up after supper, they took Wondry out the back door. Wondry raced to the bushes and sat with her back to the plants. Rhea could hear "poot-poot-poot" noises. Then Wondry crawled out and started eating the flowers on the plants.

Dad grinned. "Dessert."

Mom stood near the back door with her arms crossed and sighed as Wondry dashed from bush to bush, eating flowers.

"They'll grow back, Mom," Rhea said.

Mom smiled. "I'm sure they will. But I hope Wondry's had enough, because there won't be more for a while."

When Wondry had finished, she came toward the house and drank from the trough that they used to catch rain to water the garden. Dad opened the spout from the rain barrel to refill it.

Suddenly, Wondry ran off, out of the yard and into a little wooded area between their house and the park.

"Wondry!" Rhea called. She started to run after her, but Dad held her back. "No, stay here. You don't know where she's gone." He whistled three times: wheet! wheet! wheet! No Wondry.

"Wondry! Wondry!" Rhea shouted.

They kept calling and after a minute, Wondry bounded back into the yard. Wildflower stems dangled from her mouth. She went straight to the trough and washed her head and paws. Then she ambled over to Rhea and nudged her side.

Dad laughed. "At least she's a clean dragon."

Wondry came upstairs with Rhea at bedtime. Rhea had a double bed, all to herself. After Rhea got into bed, and her mom and dad tucked her in, Wondry carefully climbed onto the bed next to her and lay down. The dragon seemed to listen carefully while Rhea's mother read a story. When her parents left, Rhea put an arm around Wondry and they both went to sleep.

Chapter 3

The next morning was a Saturday. Dad cooked sausages and eggs on the stove while Rhea made the toast. While they were eating, Rhea noticed her father sneaking sausages to Wondry under the table.

Her mother rolled her eyes and sighed. "We'll have to make sure to get soup bones when we go grocery shopping today."

After Rhea had cleaned up after breakfast, her mother said, "You'd better take Wondry out for a while. Stay in the yard."

"See if she'll go in the bushes in the front," Dad said. "They could use some fertilizer."

Wondry followed Rhea out the front door. She thought Wondry would go right to the bushes in the yard. Instead, Wondry immediately bounded out and across the street to Eva Larson's front yard—and her prize flowers.

"Wondry, no!" Rhea shouted, running after Wondry, making sure the street was empty before she crossed. At first, she was scared that Wondry would eat all the flowers. But before she could reach Wondry, the dragon backed up into the bushes. Rhea could hear "poot-poot-poot!"

The front door opened. Eva Larson stepped outside. "What is that thing and what is it doing in my bushes?"

Rhea grabbed Wondry's collar and pulled. The dragon walked away from the bushes.

Eva Larson looked into the bushes and pointed. "You clean that up right now, young lady!"

"Yes, Ms. Larson," Rhea said. "I have to take Wondry back home, first."

"Don't ever let that . . . beast . . . in my yard again."

"Yes, Ms. Larson," Rhea answered as she pulled Wondry away. Fortunately, Wondry went with her. Rhea wondered if she was strong enough to drag Wondry if she tried to pull and Wondry did not want to go with her.

Dad met Rhea in the driveway. "What was Eva Larson yelling about?"

"Wondry went in her bushes. I have to clean it up."

"Oh," Dad reached for Wondry's collar. "I'll take Wondry inside." He nodded. "There's a bucket and a small shovel over there I use to spread manure in the garden. You can use that."

Rhea went back and scooped up Wondry's droppings to put in the bucket. When she looked both ways to cross the street again, she saw a police car slowly driving up. When she put the bucket away, she saw Officer Torres park in the driveway and get out.

Mom and Dad came out and met him. "Good morning, Officer," Dad said.

Officer Torres pointed to the Larson house. "I got a complaint from Ms. Larson that you have an unleashed animal and that it messed up her yard."

"I cleaned it up, Officer," Rhea said.

Officer Torres turned to her and smiled. "That's very nice of you, but city ordinance says that an animal has to be on a leash and in control of a human if it leaves your yard."

"Sorry, Officer," Dad said. "We just got Wondry yesterday and we're still getting used to her. It won't happen again."

"I'll just issue a warning this time," Officer Torres said, writing on a pad. He tore off a paper and gave it to Dad. "But I'd like to see the animal."

Dad nodded to Rhea, who went inside, took Wondry by the collar, and led her out. Wondry looked up at Torres curiously.

"Now that," Officer Torres said, "is an animal." He bent down, grabbed the tag on Wondry's collar, and read it. "Well, she's legal. I don't see dragons too often, though." He straightened up. "Just put a leash on her, and keep her out of trouble."

"We will, Officer. Thank you," Mom said.

Officer Torres got in the car and drove away.

"We'll need to buy a leash, too," Mom added.

They went back in the house. Mom got her purse and Dad got the shopping list.

"We'll have to lock Wondry in the garage so she won't get in trouble while we're at the store," Mom said.

"We can leave her in the house, Mom," Rhea said.

"Rhea, she might tear up the furniture while we're gone," Mom said.

"We're going to have to leave her in the house sometime," Dad said. "We won't know what she'll do until we try leaving her alone."

"She'll be good, Mom," Rhea said. "She hasn't done anything to the furniture so far."

Mom took a long look at Wondry. "We should at least close the doors to the bedrooms and closets so she won't get in there."

After she had closed all the doors, Rhea led Wondry to the blankets in the corner. She pushed the dragon's back ridges and Wondry obediently plopped down on the blankets. "Now Wondry," Rhea said, "we're going to be gone a little while, but we'll be back."

Wondry looked at her. Rhea did not know if Wondry understood or not, but Wondry did not follow her out the door.

After they went to the grocery store, they stopped at a pet shop to get a long leash and a reel that they could attach to Wondry's collar. Then Dad stopped at a farm supply store and looked around. Rhea wondered what he was looking for until he found a stack of bags of animal food with "Dragon Dinner" printed on the outside. He bought two large bags.

When they got home, Rhea rushed inside. Mom, holding a grocery bag, was right behind her. They looked in the corner. No blankets, no Wondry. Some of the dining room chairs had been moved.

"Rhea, find Wondry," Mom said, putting the bag on the table.

Rhea rushed to the living room, then ran back into the dining room. "It's okay, Mom. Wondry's in the living room, asleep."

They all hurried to the living room. Wondry had made a nest with the blankets in front of the fireplace, and was taking a nap. Nothing else in the living room had been touched.

"See Mom," Rhea said. "I told you she would be good."

They let Wondry keep her nest at the fireplace, though her water bucket stayed in the kitchen. Wondry joined them there for lunch, lying on the towels next to the water bowl as they ate. Rhea got a large wooden salad bowl from the cupboard. Dad carefully scooped some of the Dragon Dinner into the bowl for Wondry. Wondry ate all of it. Mom added a plate of soup bones, which Wondry crunched happily.

Chapter 4

The next day, Rhea put the leash on Wondry's collar.

"Now, Rhea," Mom said, "if you're going to take Wondry for a walk, you're only to go up and down this street. I don't want you turning the corner and going past Johnny Harper's place."

"But Mom, I wanted to show Wondry to Aunt LaDonna and Chantelle."

"You can go yourself and tell them if you want, but I don't want you to bring Wondry anywhere near Johnny Harper. You know what a bully he is."

"He can't hurt Wondry," Rhea said. "She's a dragon."

"Maybe," Mom said, "but if he tried to hurt Wondry, Wondry might bite him and then the police would take Wondry away."

Rhea hung her head.

"Maybe when Wondry has been with us longer, you can take her as far as Aunt LaDonna's. But not now."

"Okay Mom," Rhea said sadly. She led Wondry out to the driveway. Her father knelt by the bushes, snipping flowers. When he saw Wondry, he walked over with a handful of flowers. Wondry ate them eagerly.

"Hey, Rhea," a voice called.

They turned to see their next-door neighbor, Earl Bauer, waving at them. Mr. Bauer was a nice man. He was retired, and spent his days making things for people in his garage workshop. Rhea's mother had brought him dinner for a week after his wife passed away.

"Come over here a minute," he continued. "That's no collar for a dragon. It's all wrong. A dragon needs a harness."

"Go ahead and show Wondry to Earl," Dad said.

Mr. Bauer waved Rhea and Wondry over to a work bench. He took out a tape measure made of yellow cloth and measured Wondry around the neck and around her body in back of her legs. "What's the beast's name?"

"Wondry."

He turned back to the workbench. "I was raised on a farm. We had a couple of dragons. Ate all the mice and the foxes that tried to eat the chickens."

"Did the dragons eat the chickens?"

"No, we kept the chickens in a coop. Besides, the dragons seemed happier when they had to hunt their food." He took a thick piece of vinyl and cut it into strips. Rhea and Wondry watched curiously.

He turned to them when finished. "Now take off that leash. Pulling her by the neck doesn't work so well. It's better if the pressure is on her shoulders."

Rhea took the leash off but left the collar on. Meanwhile, he put the vinyl in a machine and pulled down on a lever. The machine put large metal staples in the vinyl.

"Now, let's see if it fits." The harness was a short strip with two long straps at each end—sort of like a capital letter "H." He put the strip between two of Wondry's neck ridges. Wondry did not seem to mind. Then he wound the straps around Wondry where her body met her front legs. "Okay," he said. "It fits." He put the harness on the workbench and turned to Rhea. "I'll be right back."

He returned carrying what seemed to be belt buckles. He stapled a buckle at the end of each strap and punched holes on the other end of each strap. "Here," he said to Rhea, "I'll show you how to put it on."

Rhea watched as he put the harness on and buckled the straps. He took it off and had Rhea do it. Wondry twisted her head to watch.

He nodded. "Good. Now attach the leash here, and you're all set." Rhea attached the leash end around the middle of the strip between Wondry's neck ridges. Once the leash was on, he added, "Remember, you walk in front of Wondry or at her side. That shows her you're the boss. If you let her walk in front, she'll think she's the boss."

"Okay, Mr. Bauer."

"If you're nice to the dragon, she'll be nice to you."

"I know, Mr. Bauer. The lady at the shelter told us."

"Well, she was right. You have what you need now."

"Thank you, Mr. Bauer." Rhea led Wondry out on Mr. Bauer's driveway and then on the sidewalk. On hot days like this, most people and pets stayed inside with the air conditioning, though Rhea and her mom and dad and Mr. Bauer never minded the heat. No one else was outside. As Rhea led her down the walk, Wondry's claws clicked on the concrete. Rhea glanced behind sometimes to see what Wondry was doing. Wondry held her head high, prancing behind her, trilling happily, turning from side to side to see the other houses. Sometimes Wondry would stop and eat the dandelions and other flowering weeds growing at the side of the road, thistles and all. They walked until Rhea saw the roof of Johnny Harper's house through the trees on the avenue. She remembered what her mother said and returned home.

Chapter 5

The next day, after Rhea's dad went to work at the computer repair store, Mom said, "I'm working at the craft shop this afternoon. Chantelle will come and stay with you until your dad gets home."

Rhea nodded. Her cousin was sixteen years old and earned money babysitting or making smartphone apps.

After breakfast, Rhea took Wondry out in the yard, where she browsed for and ate dandelions. It was pleasantly warm outside, but not hot, and she saw neighbors out in their yards. Since school was over until fall, she might have played with friends, but Naomi was at summer camp, and Isabella was on a cruise with her parents. That was one reason Rhea's parents let her have a pet.

"Come on, Wondry. Come here, girl."

Rhea turned to see Mr. Bauer kneeling in his yard, calling to Wondry. He held out a handful of flowers. Wondry trilled happily and walked over to him. Rhea followed.

While Wondry ate the flowers he offered, he patted her neck. "Good Wondry. Good girl." He looked up and saw Rhea. "I wondered if I could borrow Wondry for a while."

"What for?" Rhea asked.

Mr. Bauer waved to the garage. "Got some stones in a wagon. I've always wanted to put them around the garden in the back. I wanted Wondry to haul them for me."

"I don't know if I should let Wondry do that, Mr. Bauer."

"Aw, Wondry's strong. She could tip over a car if she wanted to."

Rhea's mouth opened in surprise.

"Come this way," he said.

Rhea followed him. Wondry followed Rhea. He had ropes tied to the wagon. Rhea already had Wondry's harness on. Mr. Bauer tied the other end of the ropes onto Wondry's harness.

"Okay, Rhea," he said. "You lead Wondry to the back yard. Unless you want to ride on Wondry."

"I can't ride on Wondry," Rhea said.

"Have you tried?" When Rhea did not answer, he explained, "I used to ride dragons all the time when I was your age. I could ride Wondry now, except she's a little too low to the ground for me."

Rhea put a hand on Wondry's side. She saw that if she grabbed one of Wondry's back ridges, she might be able to climb on Wondry's back. But she did not want to try it right now. Instead, she hooked the leash on Wondry's harness next to the ropes Mr. Bauer had tied there. She walked ahead, following Mr. Bauer to his back yard. Wondry walked behind, pulling the wagon easily. When they were there, he untied Wondry. "Thank you, Wondry. Thank you, Rhea." He started taking out rocks and put them around his garden. Wondry started eating the smaller rocks.

"No, no, Wondry," Rhea said.

"Aw, it's all right, she can have a few rocks," Mr. Bauer said.

Rhea brought Wondry in the house for lunch. She had a cheese sandwich and milk. Wondry ate more Dragon Dinner and drank a bucket of water.

After lunch, Chantelle came over and Mom went to work. Chantelle spotted Wondry sleeping in the living room. "Is that a real dragon? Cool! Can I take a picture?"

"Sure," Rhea said.

Chantelle used her smartphone to take a picture of Wondry. She showed it to Rhea. "Here. Let me take a video, too. I can send it to Dad when I talk to him tonight on my laptop."

"Is his ship still in the Pacific Ocean?" Rhea asked.

"He's not supposed to say," Chantelle said. "Sit by the dragon, Rhea, and I'll get a picture of you, too."

Rhea sat, leaning against Wondry. Wondry lifted an eye briefly and closed it again. Rhea waved at Chantelle as her cousin aimed the smartphone at her. "Hi, Uncle Roger!"

When Chantelle finished making the video, she sat on the blankets by Wondry's head. "Is it okay if I pet her?"

"Sure," Rhea said.

Chantelle stroked Wondry's head. Wondry trilled softly but did not open her eyes.

"Wow. I didn't expect a dragon to sound like that. Sounds like a tropical bird singing. What's her name?"

"Wondry. She likes to eat flowers. She's been eating all the dandelions, even the thistles."

"Say, my mom says all the flowers that have been growing around our fish pond in the back yard are just weeds. Maybe Wondry can eat those. I'll ask her."

"I have to ask my mom. I'm not supposed to take Wondry near Johnny Harper's house."

"But Wondry looks big and strong . . . oh. Your mom and dad think that if Johnny tried to hurt Wondry, Wondry would fight back and then Wondry would be in trouble."

"Uh-huh." Chantelle rubbed her chin. "Hm. Maybe your parents would let Wondry come to our house if Mom and I were with her. We'd keep Johnny away."

Chapter 6

The next evening Rhea took Wondry out for a walk. People were outdoors this time. As they walked past the Wellington house, Paula Wellington waved at them.

"Yoo hoo, Rhea! Come over here for a minute."

Rhea led Wondry to her.

Ms. Wellington bent over. "Well, aren't you a good dragon," she said to Wondry.

Wondry trilled happily.

Ms. Wellington talked to Rhea. "Earl tells me that dragon droppings make good fertilizer. I was wondering if Wondry could go in my flower bed."

"I don't know, Ms. Wellington," Rhea said. "Ms. Larson didn't like it when Wondry went in her bushes."

"Oh, Eva Larson is a grouch," she said. "Wondry is a perfectly nice dragon, aren't you, Wondry?" She scratched behind Wondry's ears. Wondry let out a satisfied, "Ooooooo."

"You can bring Wondry to my house anytime," Ms. Wellington continued.

Rhea looked at the Wellington's flower bed. "Wondry might eat your flowers."

"Oh, that's okay," Ms. Wellington said. "She can eat a few flowers."

"She might eat all of them, I mean."

Ms. Wellington rubbed her chin. "Hm." She looked around the lawn. Flowers were everywhere. "Then just let her loose by the flower bushes in the front. Those are just for me. She can have those if she wants. I can scoop up the fertilizer and carry it to the flower bed with my prize flowers. There's a fence around those."

Rhea led Wondry to the flower bushes. Sure enough, Wondry began to eat the flowers there. But she only ate flowers from one of the bushes before she turned around. "Poot-poot-poot."

When Wondry was done, Rhea led her toward the road again.

Ms. Wellington looked at the mound of droppings. "That's wonderful! Thank you, Rhea. Thank you, Wondry. Come back anytime."

Rhea continued down the street. They passed people walking dogs. Some of the dogs barked at Wondry. Wondry craned her neck to look at them and went "trrryl, trrryl, trrryl." The dogs stopped barking. Their owners pulled them away. Little kids came up to Wondry and hugged her neck. Wondry went, "Ooooooo, ooooooo, ooooooo." Grownups pushed strollers with babies in them. Most of them pushed the strollers around Wondry when Rhea and Wondry approached. One mother stopped and let Wondry sniff her baby. The baby gurgled at Wondry and waved its arms. Wondry said, "Oooooooo," and the baby giggled.

They walked some more, and just ahead of them, some wild geese from the park waddled across a lawn and onto the sidewalk. Wondry saw them and crouched low to the ground. Her head and neck were just inches from the sidewalk and when Rhea looked back, she saw Wondry holding her tail just above the sidewalk, too.

Slowly, Wondry crept toward the geese. Rhea turned from side to side to see if anyone else was close. She was not sure what would happen if Wondry ate a goose and people saw it. Most of the neighbors thought the geese were a nuisance. They left icky green droppings all over the sidewalk and made a lot of noise.

The geese did not seem to see Wondry coming. They were waddling away from her. Rhea kept a tight hold on Wondry's leash in case Wondry tried to bolt, even though she doubted that she could hold on to Wondry if Wondry ran.

Wondry's head drew almost even to the tail feathers of the last goose in line.

"Guggle-guggle-guggle-guggle!"

Rhea jumped, startled by the sudden noise coming from deep within Wondry's throat. The geese, frightened, honked loudly and flew away. Wondry stretched her neck upwards and called after them.

"Guggle-guggle-guggle-guggle!"

When the geese were far away, Wondry again strutted beside Rhea. The dragon seemed very proud of herself for scaring them away.

At the end of the block, Rhea turned around to walk back home. Just across the street, a car with a boat on a trailer turned the corner. A cat ran in front of the car and the driver swerved. The car missed the cat but the trailer tipped over with a crash. The boat had been clamped to the trailer and did not fall off.

The driver stopped and got out of the car. "Is everyone all right?"

"Yes, Mr. Johnson," Rhea said.

Grant Johnson sighed and looked at the trailer. "I guess I'll have to get some neighbors to help me get it right side up again."

Already, the neighbors were running up to help. Mr. Bauer pointed to Wondry. "Wondry, here, can help you." He waved to Rhea. "Bring Wondry over here." Rhea led Wondry to the overturned trailer. Wondry squirmed underneath the boat. Mr. Bauer directed other grownups to stand at either end of the boat. "Now," he said, "Wondry will do most of the work, but you'll need to steady the boat and push too." He bent down and patted Wondry's stomach. "Okay, girl, up!"

Wondry let out a snort and stood. The boat and trailer flipped upright. Grownups steadied it as it rocked back and forth slightly. Wondry stretched her neck proudly as the neighbors applauded.

Rhea hugged Wondry. "Good Wondry."

"Thank you," Mr. Johnson said. "Is there anything I can get you?"

"You can get Wondry a bouquet of flowers," Mr. Bauer said.

"I will." Mr. Johnson got back in his car, waved, and drove off. The neighbors walked back to their homes.

That evening, Mr. Johnson rang their doorbell and presented Wondry with a huge bouquet of roses, which Wondry devoured happily, thorns and all.

Chapter 7

The summer week dragged on. While Rhea missed her friends, she loved playing with Wondry. One afternoon, Mom gave Rhea some money so she could get ice cream from the truck and buy Wondry flowers from the cart. Rhea walked Wondry to the park, where she bought a chocolate ice cream bar right away. The woman who sold flowers stood nearby. Rhea bought a bunch for Wondry and led Wondry to a bench. She sat and ate while Wondry lay at her feet nibbling the flowers. No one was nearby.

Suddenly, a rock struck Wondry. Rhea looked up to see Johnny Harper standing across the street from them. He had rocks in his hand, and threw another at Wondry. This one, too, bounced off Wondry's tough hide. Wondry searched for the rocks on the ground and ate them. Johnny threw another rock and Wondry chased after it, as if it were a game to her.

"Stop that!" Rhea said.

"Who's going to stop me?" Johnny sneered. He was a teenager, thin and much taller than Rhea. His yellowish-brown hair hung over his eyes.

Rhea looked around for the park patrol but did not see anyone.

He threw another rock. Wondry found it and ate it. "Do you know what you do with dragons?"

"Mr. Bauer says you are supposed to be nice to them."

"You're supposed to slay them." He threw another rock. "At home, I have a sword, and I'm going to slay your dragon."

Rhea stood and faced him. "You are not!"

He threw another rock, which again bounced off Wondry. "Are too!"

Johnny was interrupted by a line of cars driving by, between them. Rhea guessed that the baseball game at the other end of the park had ended. When the cars continued to come, Johnny walked away.

Rhea sat back on the bench, thinking. Wondry was tough and strong, but what if someone tried to chop her head off? Could Johnny do it? She wondered if she could ask Mr. Bauer, but then he would ask why. She definitely could not tell her parents. She would get into trouble if she said she had talked to Johnny.

Wondry, after looking around and finding no more rocks to eat, came up to Rhea and put her head on Rhea's lap. Rhea patted Wondry's head and stroked Wondry's neck. Somehow, Rhea felt stronger when Wondry was around, as if Wondry's strength made her braver. She would not let Johnny hurt Wondry. But she needed a plan. What would she do if Johnny came up to her with a sword? She would run away. Wondry could run away. She never saw anyone run as fast as Wondry. She remembered that first night when Wondry ran out of the yard—Wondry had been gone in a flash. Johnny could never catch Wondry if she ran.

He might, however, catch up with Rhea. She ran fast in gym class, but knew that when she

and her father raced in the park, she only got ahead when her father let her.

Wondry let out a happy "Ooooooo, ooooooo, ooooooo" as Rhea continued to pet her.

Then Rhea remembered that Mr. Bauer said that she should be able to ride Wondry. If she could, hanging on to Wondry's collar, they could get away from Johnny. But would Wondry let Rhea on her back? There was only one way to find out.

With Wondry's leash still in her hand, Rhea walked to Wondry's shoulder. Wondry craned her neck to watch. Rhea looked at Wondry's back ridges. The spaces between them were wide enough for her to sit between them. She should be able to sit on Wondry's back if she wanted to.

She turned to Wondry's head and said, "I'm going to get on your back, okay?" She did not know if Wondry understood, but when she grabbed a ridge, Wondry did not protest. Holding the ridge, she swung a leg up and around, and found Wondry pushing her up with her head. Then she knew that this must be all right with Wondry.

With one hand on the leash, and the other on the ridge in front of her, Rhea sat, without moving, on Wondry's back for a minute. Wondry still had her head swung around, looking at her. Rhea felt very safe on Wondry's back. She did not feel at all as if she might slip off.

"Okay, Wondry, go ahead."

Wondry swung her head around again and began to walk. Rhea rocked back and forth as Wondry moved, but again, she did not feel as if she were going to fall off. Wondry walked faster, trotting, and once more Rhea did not feel as if she might slip. Rhea smiled. If Johnny tried to hurt Wondry, she knew they could run away together now.

Chapter 8

The next day, Rhea's father came home before her mother. Her mother promised to bring pizza for supper. While they were waiting, her father decided to mow the lawn.

"Now, you hold on to Wondry," Dad said to Rhea as he rolled out the mower. "We don't know what she'll do."

"Okay, Dad."

Wondry watched the mower curiously as Rhea held on to her collar. When Dad climbed into the seat and started the engine, Wondry stomped her feet excitedly. Dad drove the mower on the lawn. Grass clippings came out of the side. Wondry leaned forward, but Rhea held on to her. "No, Wondry, you're not supposed to run up to the mower," she shouted over the engine noise.

Dad noticed Wondry getting excited and waved at Rhea to let Wondry go. When she did, Wondry ran toward the mower and then around it. The dragon almost danced on the lawn, prancing up and down, letting the mower shower her with grass clippings.

Dad had almost finished the lawn when Mom drove into the driveway. She stopped the car, got out holding a pizza box, and watched Wondry for a minute. Then she took the pizza into the house. When she came out again, Dad had turned off the engine and rolled the mower onto the driveway.

"Rhea," Dad said, "you're going to have to take a hose and wash the grass clippings off Wondry before you bring her in the house."

"Okay, Dad."

With the mower off, Wondry became calm again and walked up to Rhea. Rhea turned on the water, grabbed the hose, and pointed the nozzle at the end of the hose at Wondry. All Rhea had to do was to push on the lever and the water sprayed on Wondry. Wondry seemed to think this was fun. She opened her mouth and tried to drink the water as Rhea walked around her to wash off the grass clippings. Once Wondry was clean, Rhea pointed the hose at Wondry's mouth and let her have a long drink.

"Be sure to pick up her tail and wash underneath," Dad called.

Rhea picked up Wondry's tail and sprayed that part as Wondry craned her neck and watched. Rhea made sure to wash Wondry's tail as well. Mom threw Rhea an old towel to dry Wondry off as Dad took the hose and turned off the water. Wondry trilled happily as Rhea rubbed her with the towel.

Later, the Monroes sat at the table and ate their pizza while Wondry munched on her Dragon Dinner.

Mom said, "Wondry's been a good dragon, and she seems to be smart, as well. Let's see if we can train Wondry to stay still."

Dad smiled. "You mean teach her to sit?"

"Like a dog?" Rhea asked.

Mom nodded. "At least let's see if we can get her to obey *sit* and *stay*."

"How about *fetch*?" Dad asked.

Mom sighed and rolled her eyes. Dad chuckled.

After dinner, they took Wondry out on the driveway. Rhea stood facing Wondry. "Okay, Wondry. Sit!" She bent her knees and sat on the driveway. Wondry rested her backside and tail on the cement.

"Good Wondry!" Rhea stood and patted Wondry on the head. She backed away from Wondry. "Now. Stay!"

Wondry got up and started to follow.

Rhea stopped. "Wondry, sit!"

Wondry stopped and sat again.

Rhea patted Wondry. "Good girl! Now, stay."

"Hold on!" Dad called. "Before you back off, let your mother and me hold Wondry. Maybe she'll get the message."

Rhea watched while Dad and Mom stood on either side of Wondry, hanging on to her collar.

Rhea pointed at Wondry. "Wondry, stay!" She started to back away.

Wondry stood and raised a leg to step forward, but Dad and Mom pulled her back. Wondry turned her head to look at Dad, and then Mom, and sat again.

"Good Wondry!" Rhea called.

Dad and Mom patted Wondry. "Good Wondry!"

Wondry trilled. She seemed pleased with herself.

Rhea backed away again. "Stay, Wondry, stay."

This time Wondry watched as Rhea walked backward. When Dad and Mom let go of her collar, Wondry remained still as Rhea backed all the way to the garage.

"Good Wondry!" Rhea said.

"Now call her and see if she'll come," Mom suggested.

Rhea clapped her hands and waved at Wondry. "Wondry, come!"

Wondry turned from Mom to Dad, then bounded up to Rhea. Rhea patted Wondry's head and neck. "Good Wondry!"

Dad went to the recycling box and took out a newspaper. He pulled out a big page and wadded it into a ball. Then he threw the ball on the lawn. "Wondry, fetch."

Wondry sat on the driveway and watched the paper ball, but did nothing.

Dad took another sheet of paper and crumpled it. He threw that onto the lawn, too. "Wondry, *fetch*."

Wondry again watched Dad throw the ball, but did nothing.

"Look, Wondry." He made another paper ball, threw it out on the lawn, ran after it, picked it up, and brought it back to Wondry. He dropped it at her feet. "See?"

Wondry hit the paper ball with her tail. It sailed into the air.

Dad caught it. He looked surprised at first, then he smiled and threw the ball toward Wondry's tail. Again, Wondry hit the ball with her tail. Dad grabbed it. He laughed. "It seems that Wondry has more fun playing *catch* than *fetch*."

"I guess that's what dragons do, Dad," Rhea said.

"We're learning more about Wondry all the time, aren't we?" Dad said.

Rhea smiled and nodded. "I bet Wondry can do a lot of things we don't know about yet."

"I bet she can, too," Dad said.

Chapter 9

Rhea's parents waited until Saturday before letting Rhea take Wondry to Chantelle's house. Aunt LaDonna came with Chantelle to walk with them. They arrived just as Rhea was buckling on Wondry's harness. Rhea put that on whenever she and Wondry left the house but took it off again whenever they came home.

"What a nice looking dragon," Aunt LaDonna said. She patted Wondry's head. Wondry trilled happily. "What a pleasant sound. It's almost as if Wondry were singing."

"I'm glad you came," Mom said. "I don't want that Johnny Harper getting anywhere near Wondry."

Aunt LaDonna nodded. "I have cameras around the house and told him that if he even steps in our yard, I'm taking the video to the police. I've told his mother, too, but she thinks Johnny never does anything bad and people who complain about him are making it up."

Chantelle rubbed Wondry behind an ear. "We'll take care of Wondry, Aunt Heather."

"I'll be glad to have Wondry visit," Aunt LaDonna said. "Every year, it seems we get more weeds by the fish pond. We dig them up and they just come back again. The geese have been visiting too. We put up nets to keep them away."

"They're a nuisance for just about everyone," Mom said.

"If seeing Wondry around keeps the geese away, that will be fine with me," Aunt LaDonna said.

"Mr. Bauer says she scared all the squirrels out of his yard," Rhea volunteered.

Aunt LaDonna turned to Rhea. "Good for Wondry."

Mom turned to Rhea and hugged her. "Make sure you do what Aunt LaDonna tells you."

Rhea sighed. "I always do, Mom."

They walked to Aunt LaDonna's house with Chantelle and Rhea in the front. Wondry trailed behind and Aunt LaDonna stayed next to Wondry. When they turned the corner, they looked in the Harpers' yard. No one was there.

"Looks like Johnny's not there, Mom," Chantelle said.

"Let's hope it stays that way," Aunt LaDonna answered.

When they reached Aunt LaDonna's house, she told Rhea and Chantelle to let Wondry browse all she wanted. "As long as Wondry eats the flowering weeds, she can have any of the other flowers in our yard if she wants them."

"Wondry might go in the bushes," Rhea said.

Aunt LaDonna smiled. "That's all right. They can use the fertilizer." She went inside.

Rhea took off the harness. Wondry went in the bushes then ate all the weedy wildflowers around the fish pond, along with some dirt and stones. Uncle Roger and Aunt LaDonna had built the fish pond. It was a shallow rocky bowl filled with water and goldfish. A purple net had been spread over it. Rhea thought the net looked pretty too. Three smaller pottery bowls around the fish pond caught extra water when it rained. Wondry drank from the smaller bowls. Chantelle said that was okay and got a hose and refilled them.

Chantelle took Rhea and Wondry inside. Rhea liked Aunt LaDonna's house. On the wall were pictures of Uncle Roger in his uniform, pictures of Aunt LaDonna when she was a Marine, and pictures of Chantelle holding her science fair awards. Rhea knew that Chantelle hoped she could get into a service academy.

Chantelle turned her game player on. She and Rhea sat in the living room playing a video game while Wondry sat between them, her head in Rhea's lap. Wondry did not seem to mind the video game noise. She fell asleep after a while.

Suddenly, they heard honking. Wondry woke up and raised her head.

Aunt LaDonna called out, "Geese!"

Chantelle put her video control down. "Come on, Rhea, let's bring Wondry."

They let Wondry out in the back yard. When Wondry chased them, going "guggle-guggle-guggle," a lot of the geese flew off. One ran away. Wondry ran after that one and knocked over a small pottery bowl as she did.

"We'll get it," Aunt LaDonna said to Rhea. "You go get Wondry."

Rhea hurried around the house into the front yard, where a goose honked while running away from Wondry. The goose flapped its wings but did not get off the ground. Wondry kept after the goose, which ran across the street toward the Harper house. Although no one was in the yard, Rhea did not want Wondry there.

"Wondry, sit!" Rhea called.

Wondry sat near the end of Aunt LaDonna's front yard, close to the sidewalk. The goose flapped into the air and flew off.

Rhea rushed over to Wondry and grabbed her collar. She did not want Wondry to get into the street where she might be hit by a car.

At that moment, Johnny Harper charged out of his house, yelling, holding a sword above his head. He ran straight to Wondry and Rhea, crossing the street without even looking for cars.

Rhea was about to climb on Wondry's back so they could scamper away when Wondry pulled loose from Rhea's grip. Wondry set her tail on the ground and lifted her front paws. She stretched her neck up as far as it would go. She looked about ten feet tall. Then she lowered her head until she was facing Johnny and let out a roar.

Rhea had not heard such a loud noise since she heard the jets take off at the airport. The windows in the nearby houses shook.

Then there was silence. Rhea had never heard the neighborhood so quiet before.

Johnny turned around and ran back to his house. Rhea could see his pants were wet and he smelled bad as if he had gone in his shorts. He cried like a baby. The sword was still in his hand, but now he dragged it behind him.

Wondry put her feet back down on the ground and ate a dandelion.

Rhea heard sirens. Lots of sirens. Wondry raised her head and stamped her feet excitedly. Rhea remembered what her mom said about Wondry getting into trouble and the police taking her away. She grabbed Wondry's collar and pulled. "Come, Wondry." Rhea wanted to get Wondry in Aunt LaDonna's garage.

Chantelle came up to them and held flowers in front of Wondry's nose. "Come on, Wondry. Come on, girl. See what I have? Flowers. Yummy, yummy flowers. Yummy flowers for dragon."

Wondry began to move. Chantelle held the flowers just out of Wondry's reach until they got to Aunt LaDonna's open garage. The sirens got louder.

Johnny's mother stomped out of her house and pointed at Wondry. "Don't you run away! I've called the police, and they're coming to get that dangerous animal."

Meanwhile, Chantelle had given Wondry the flowers. Wondry munched them happily.

Aunt LaDonna appeared from the back yard. "They'll do no such thing, Alice Harper! Mind your own business!"

The sirens got even louder. People from the neighborhood had run toward the noise. A crowd was gathering.

"We'll see what the police say!" Ms. Harper yelled.

Three police cars came around the corner, two from one direction, and one from another direction. They met at the intersection and stopped. The sirens turned off, but the lights flashed.

Rhea hugged Wondry. No one was going to take away her dragon.

Chapter 10

Police officers stepped out of their cars. Rhea saw Officer Torres, two other men officers, and two women officers.

Ms. Harper pointed to Wondry. "That beast attacked my son!"

"Oh, hush up, Alice," said Mr. Bauer, who had just arrived and joined the crowd.

"We need to talk to anyone who saw anything," Officer Torres said. "The rest of you folks can go on home."

"We heard a loud noise," Ms. Wellington said.

"So did everyone within a mile of here," one of the women officers said.

Rhea's parents rushed into Aunt LaDonna's yard and went straight to Rhea. "Are you all right?" Dad asked.

Rhea nodded without letting go of Wondry or taking her eyes of the police officers.

Aunt LaDonna leaned toward Mom. "I need to go into the house for a moment."

"How many of you actually saw something?" Officer Torres asked in a voice loud enough for anyone to hear.

Rhea raised a hand. No one else did, not even Alice Harper.

"All right, the rest of you folks can go on home," Officer Torres said. "We'll take care of things."

"Can't keep us from visiting with our neighbors, officer," Mr. Bauer said.

Officer Torres sighed. "All right, but stay out of the way." The other officers motioned everyone to step back.

Officer Torres turned to Ms. Harper. "I take it you didn't see anything, ma'am?"

"My son came in the house a mess and said that the dragon attacked him."

"And where's your son?"

"He's changing. He'll be out soon."

"We'll need to talk to him, then. Just stay where you are for now."

Officer Torres walked up the driveway until he was a couple of steps away from Rhea and Wondry. He knelt in front of Rhea and took out a notepad. "Why don't you tell me what happened?"

Rhea wondered what to tell him. What if the officer took Wondry away?

Mom bent down. "It's all right, Rhea. Just tell the officer what you saw."

Wondry nudged Rhea playfully and trilled. Rhea felt better. She took a breath. "Wondry was chasing a goose and I told her to sit, so she did. Johnny came out of the house with a sword."

Officer Torres paused in writing. "A sword, you said?"

Rhea nodded. "He was yelling and screaming."

"What did he say?"

"Nothing. He was just making yelling and screaming noises."

"What happened then?"

"He ran toward me and Wondry. Wondry stood up on her hind legs and roared. Then Johnny turned around and went home."

"Did Johnny hurt you or Wondry?"

"No."

"Did Wondry bite Johnny?"

"No, she just roared at him."

"Did she scratch him?"

"No, she just roared at him," Rhea repeated.

"Did Wondry touch him at all?"

"No, Officer."

Aunt LaDonna stepped up and held up a flash drive. "My security cameras caught it all." She turned to Chantelle. "Let me borrow your smartphone." She inserted the flash drive into the phone's adapter and played the video for Officer Torres. Wondry's roar was faint when heard through the smartphone speaker, but Wondry trilled at hearing her own voice. Then Aunt LaDonna took the flash drive out and handed it to the officer.

"Okay," Officer Torres said. "You folks just stay here and stand by. I'll come right back." He walked to Alice Harper in her yard.

Rhea kept her arm around Wondry. Officer Torres had not sounded angry. He had not said anything about taking Wondry.

Chantelle turned to Aunt LaDonna. "They aren't going to do anything to Wondry, are they?"

Aunt LaDonna crossed her arms in front of her. "Not if I have anything to say about it."

Across the street, Johnny walked out into his yard, wearing new clothes and not carrying his sword. Officer Torres approached him and his mother. The officer also had a smartphone and adapter. He put Aunt LaDonna's flash drive in it and showed it to them.

"You see!" Ms. Harper said. "That dragon attacked my son, just as I said."

Officer Torres turned to Johnny. "Is this what happened?"

"Yes, that is exactly what happened. I was defending myself from that dragon."

"What did the dragon do that you had to defend yourself?"

"It's a dangerous animal," Ms. Harper said.

"I was asking your son, ma'am," Officer Torres said.

"It was charging me," Johnny said.

"Looks to me like it was sitting quietly and *you* did the charging," Officer Torres pointed to the picture on the screen. "Is that your sword?"

"Yes, it is," Johnny said.

"Is it a toy sword or a real sword with a sharp edge?" Officer Torres asked.

"It's a real sword. It's very sharp," Johnny said proudly.

Officer Torres put the smartphone and flash drive away. He took out handcuffs. "Then you are under arrest for assault with a deadly weapon. Put your hands behind your back, please."

"What?" Ms. Harper shouted.

Johnny obeyed the officer. His mouth was open. He seemed stunned. Officer Torres put him in the back of his squad car.

One of the women officers turned to Ms. Harper. "You can ride to the station with me if you want. I'll go in the house with you to get the sword."

"This is ridiculous!" Ms. Harper said.

"You can talk to the public defender," Officer Torres said, "but he's coming with us." He turned to Dad and Mom. "Are you willing to press charges on behalf of your daughter?"

"Yes," they said at the same time.

"I'm pressing charges for trespassing," Aunt LaDonna said. "Johnny was clearly in my yard."

Officer Torres tipped his hat. "Yes, ma'am. We'll be in touch." He got in the car and drove away. Ms. Harper went in her house with the woman officer. They came out with the officer holding the sword, which was now in a sheath. They got into the second police car and left. The third car followed them.

When the police cars were gone, the neighbors all cheered and applauded. Then they crowded into Aunt LaDonna's driveway.

"Hooray for Wondry!" Mr. Bauer said.

"Hooray for Rhea, too," Aunt LaDonna said. "She kept Wondry in the yard, stayed calm, and answered the officer's questions."

All the other neighbors wanted to pet Wondry or tell Rhea how brave she had been. Some thanked her.

Eventually, the neighbors went back to their homes. Rhea turned to Dad and Mom. "So, no one is going to take Wondry away?"

"No one would let anyone take Wondry away after this," Dad said.

Rhea hugged Wondry. "You're ours for good, now, Wondry."

Wondry trilled happily.

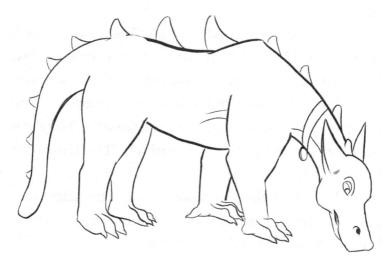

Made in the USA
Monee, IL
06 February 2024